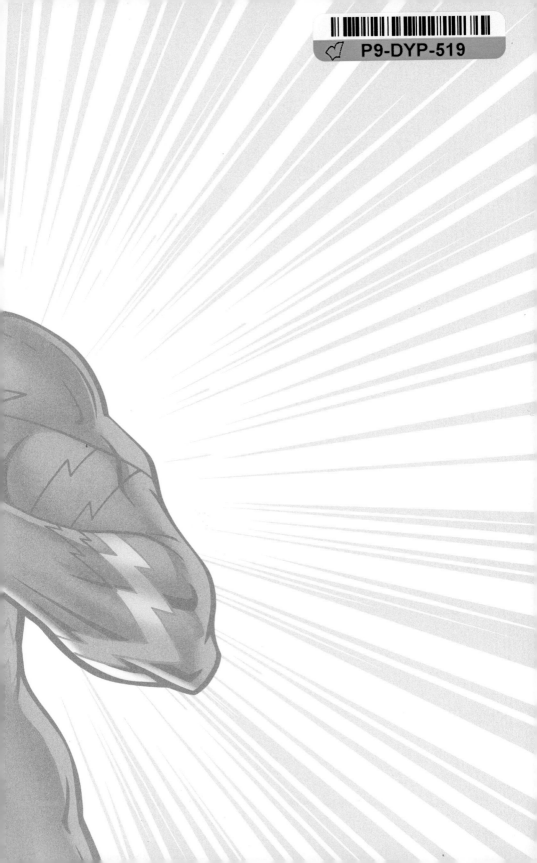

HOW FAST IS THE FLASH?

Written by Vicky Armstrong

Editor Vicky Armstrong
Project Art Editor Stefan Georgiou
Senior Production Editor Jennifer Murray
Senior Production Controller Mary Slater
Managing Editors Emma Grange, Sarah Harland
Managing Art Editor Vicky Short
Publishing Director Mark Searle

Proofreader Kayla Dugger
Reading Consultant Barbara Marinak

First American Edition, 2021
Published in the United States by DK Publishing
1450 Broadway, Suite 801, New York, NY 10018

Page design copyright © 2021 Dorling Kindersley Limited
DK, a Division of Penguin Random House LLC
21 22 23 24 25 10 9 8 7 6 5 4 3 2 1
001–323483–Dec/2021

A catalog record for this book is available from the Library of Congress.

PB ISBN 978-0-7440-3982-5
HB ISBN 978-0-7440-3983-2

DK books are available at special discounts when purchased in bulk
for sales promotions, premiums, fund-raising, or educational use.
For details, contact: DK Publishing Special Markets,
1450 Broadway, Suite 801, New York, NY 10018
SpecialSales@dk.com

Printed and bound in China

For the curious

www.dk.com

MIX
Paper from
responsible sources
FSC™ C018179

This book was made with Forest Stewardship
Council ™ certified paper—one small step in
DK's commitment to a sustainable future.
For more information go to
www.dk.com/our-green-pledge

Contents

Meet Barry Allen

Barry Allen lives in Central City. He works as a forensic scientist at the Central City Police Department. He is very clever, and he loves chemistry. He is also very relaxed. This makes him late for everything.

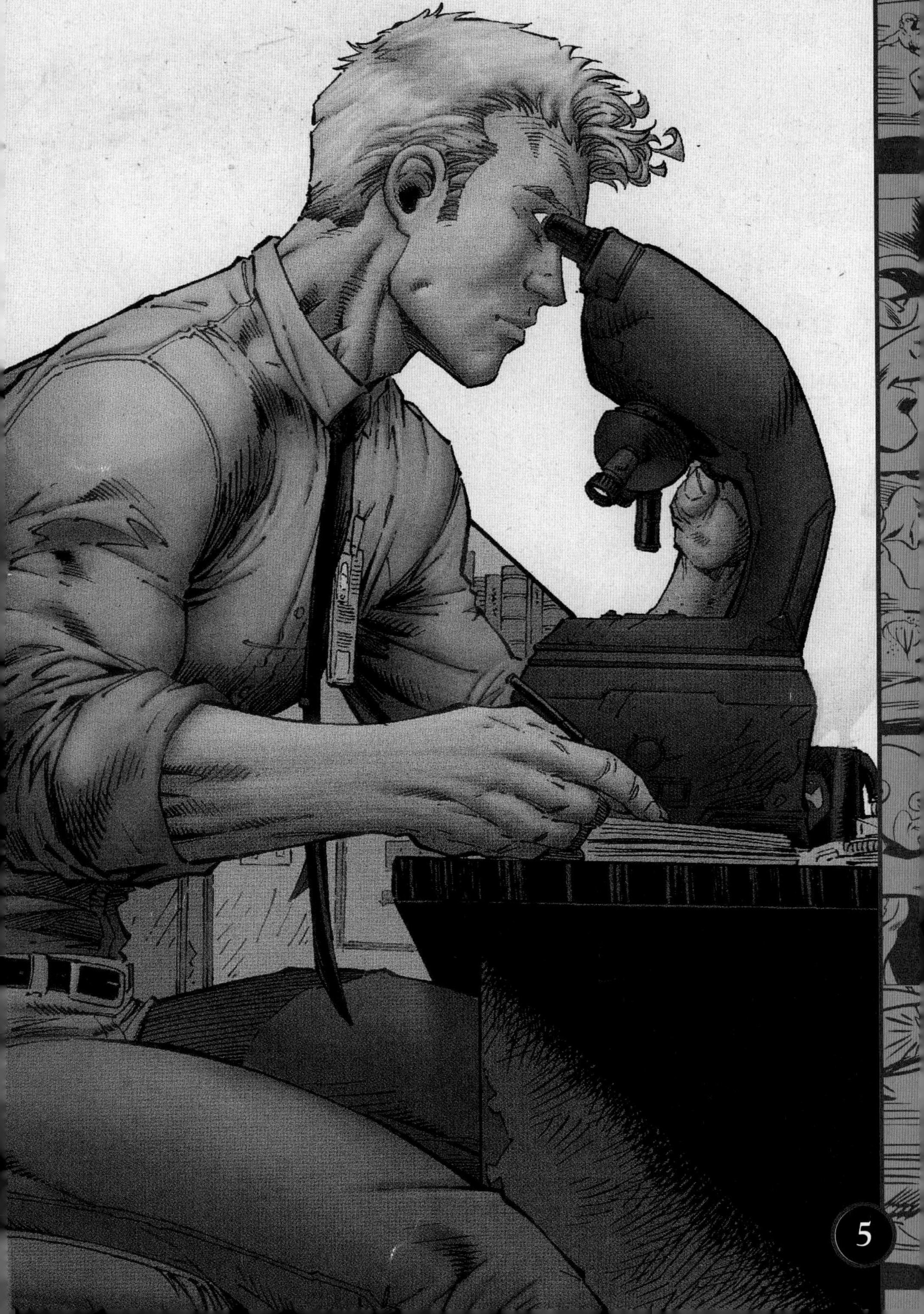

Family life

Barry had a sad childhood. His mother was killed when he was a young boy. Barry's father was sent to prison for the crime, and Barry went to live with a family friend.

Barry spent a lot of time trying to prove that his father was innocent. Barry decided to work for the police department when he grew up. He wanted to help other people like him.

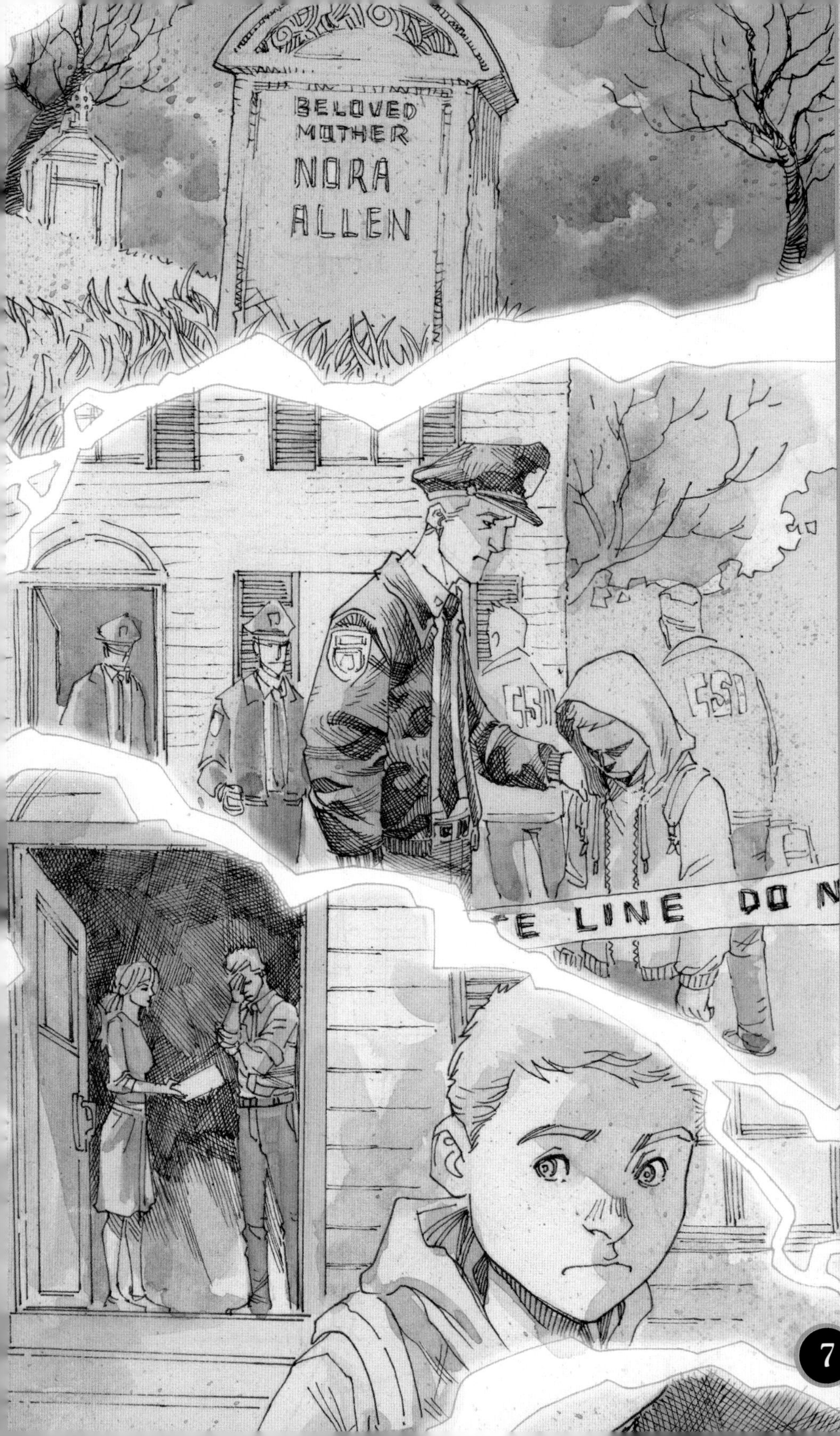
BELOVED MOTHER NORA ALLEN
E LINE DO N

One fateful day

Barry is working in his laboratory one night during a big storm. A bolt of lightning hits and smashes his bottles of chemicals. Barry is covered in the chemicals and faints. When Barry wakes up, he realizes he has superpowers! Barry now needs a Super Hero name. He decides to call himself The Flash.

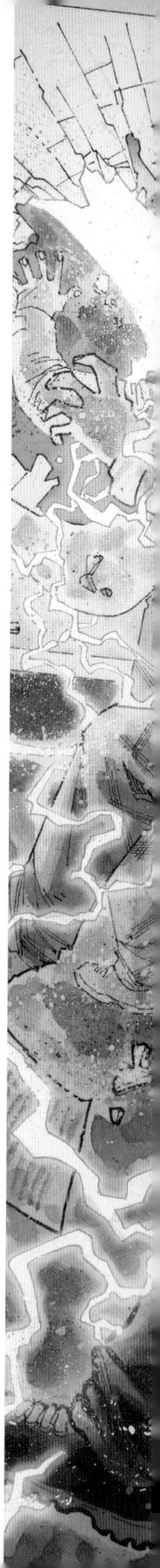

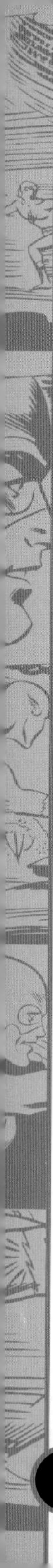

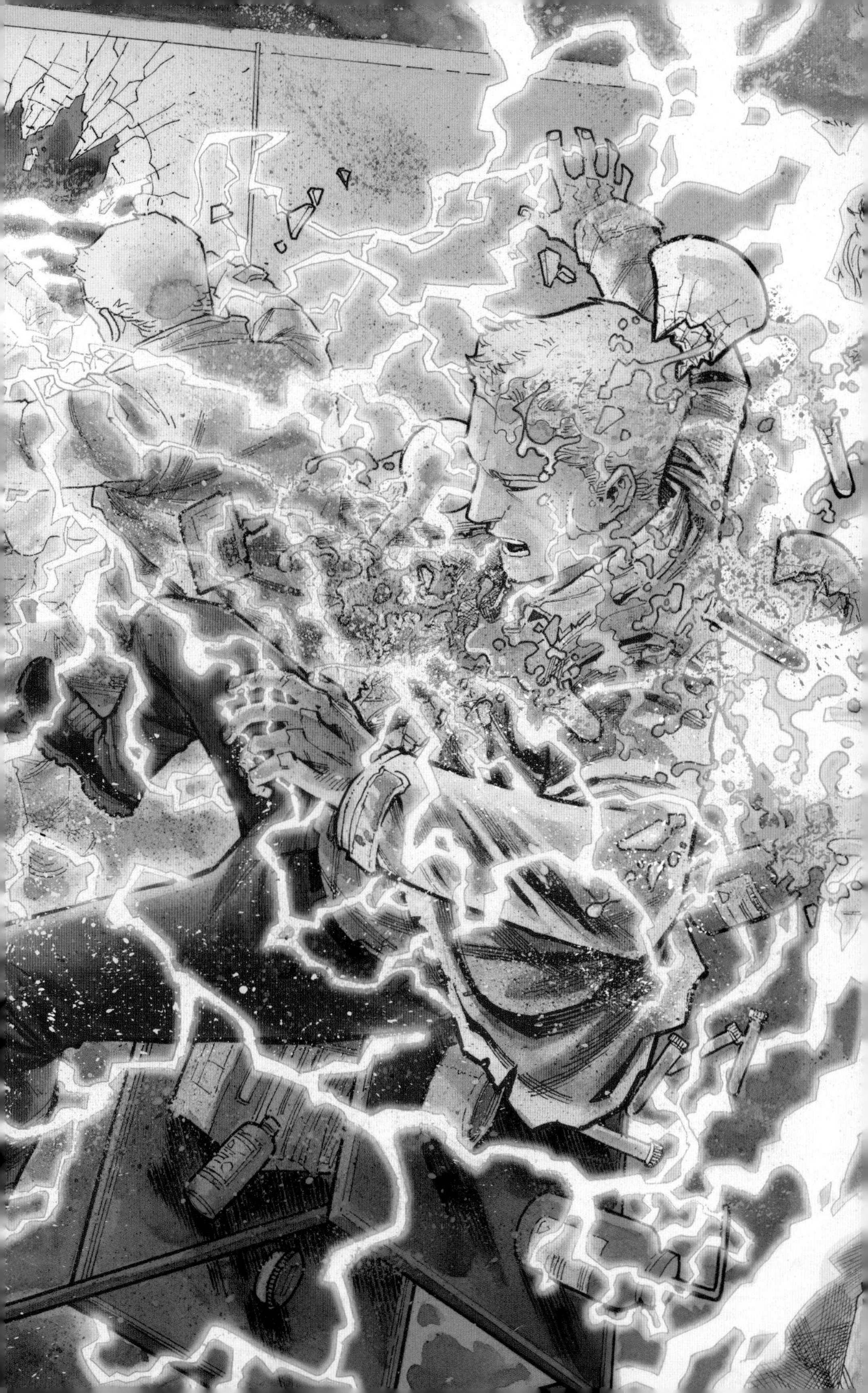

The Flash

The Flash's super-speed powers mean that he can move incredibly fast. Sometimes, he is so fast that he is a blur. He can travel at super-speed for a long time without becoming tired.

The Flash has superhuman agility. He can also heal much faster than a normal person when he hurts himself.

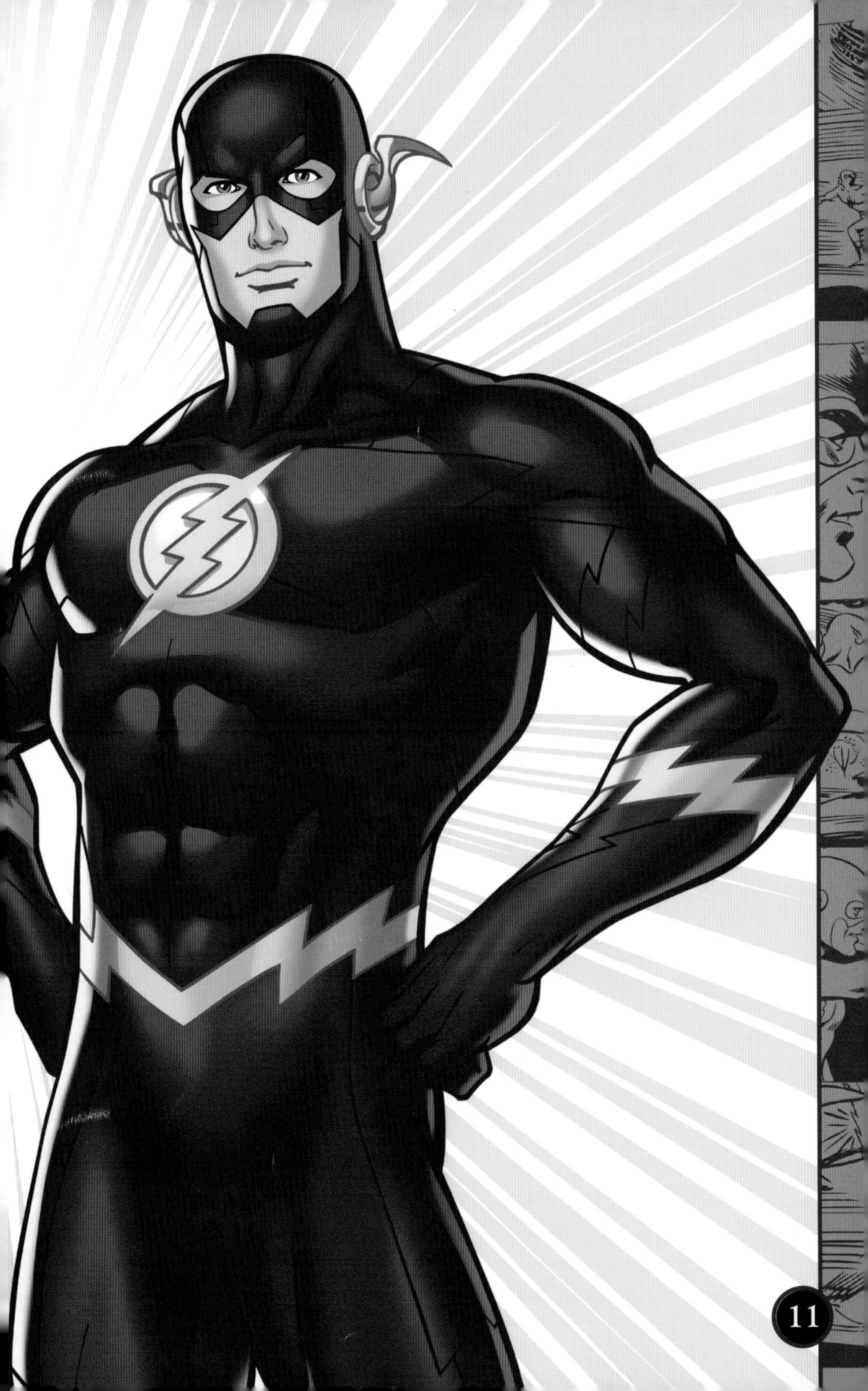

Central City

Central City is across the
river from Keystone City.
There is a lot of crime
in Central City—it
needs a Super Hero!
The Flash decides to use
his new powers to make
Central City a better place.

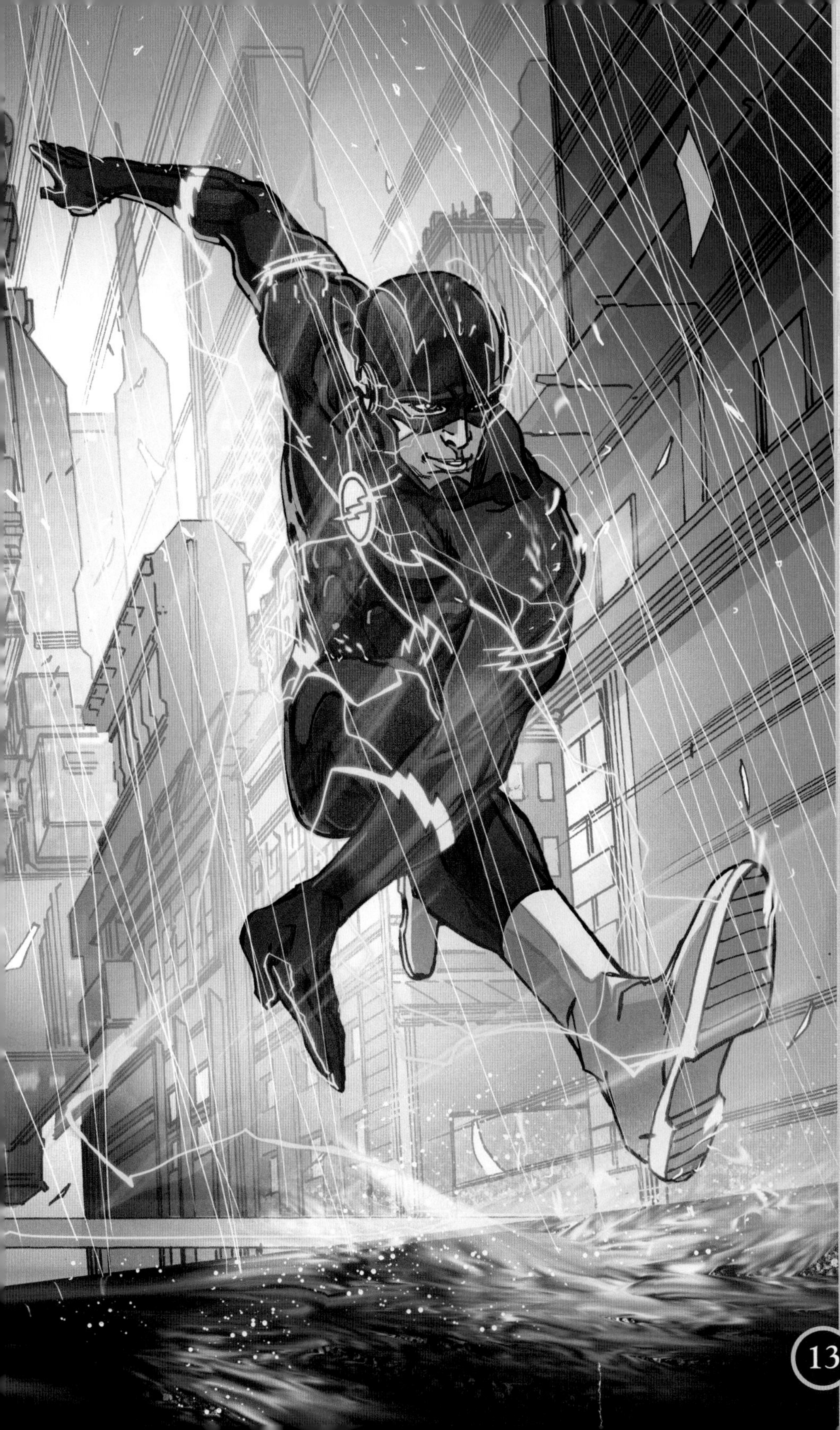

The Speed Force

The Speed Force gives The Flash his super-speed powers. It is an energy source, like the sun.

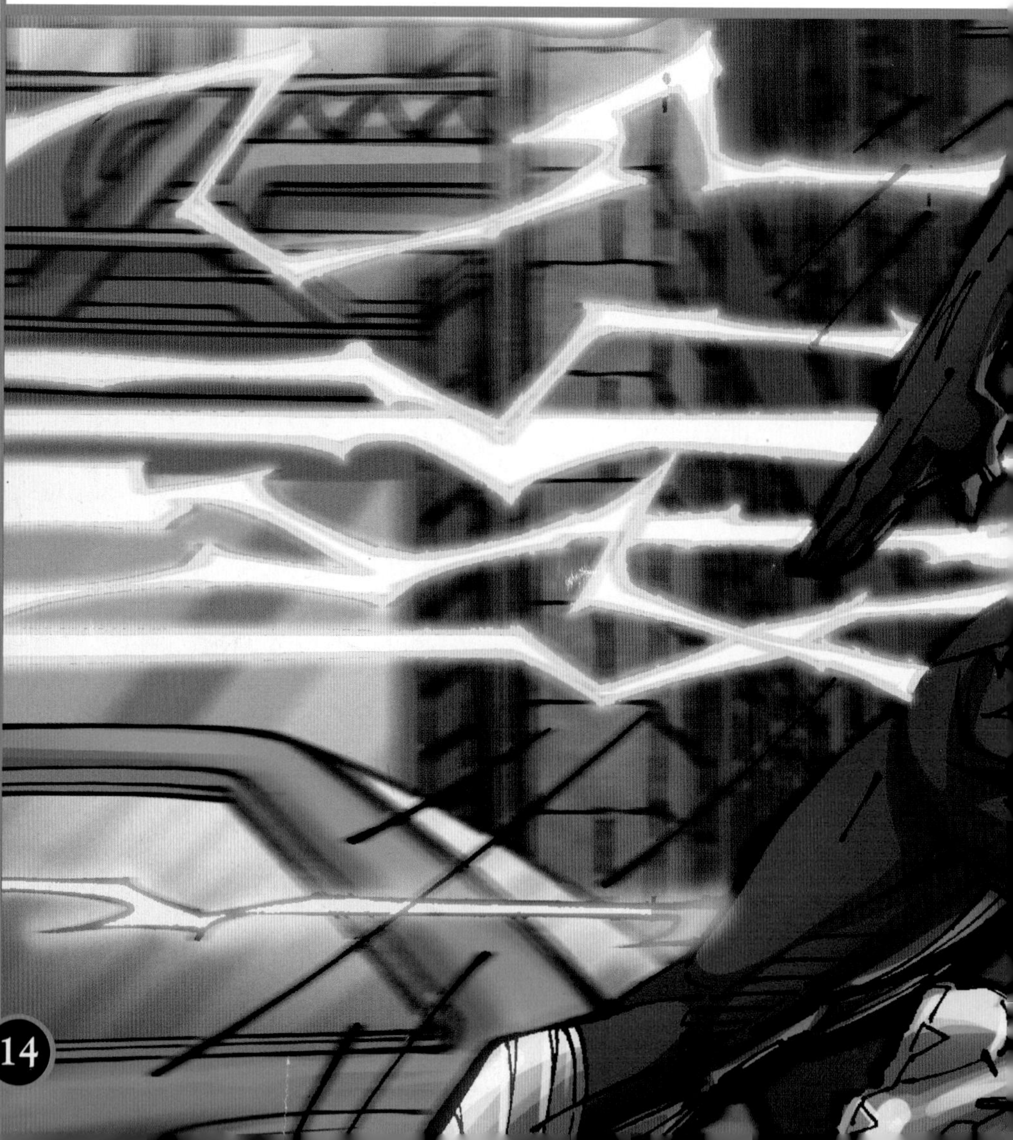

When speedsters like The Flash run, they help reduce the pressure of the Speed Force. This stops huge disasters from happening.

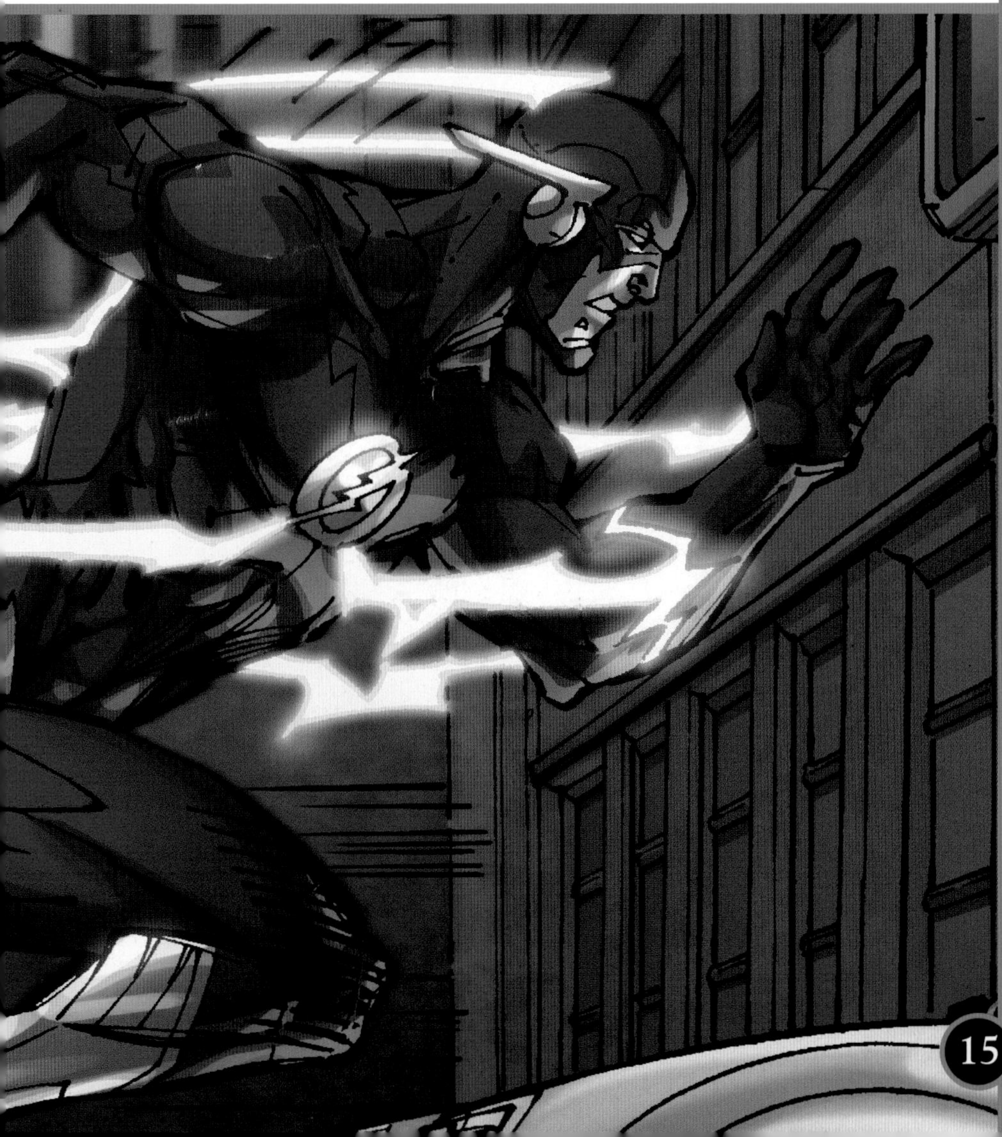

The Flash suit

Lots of Super Heroes wear
a costume when they are
fighting crime and
protecting people.

Barry designed this
suit himself. It hides
his identity. It also
protects him when
he is traveling
at super-speed.

Costume
ring to
store suit

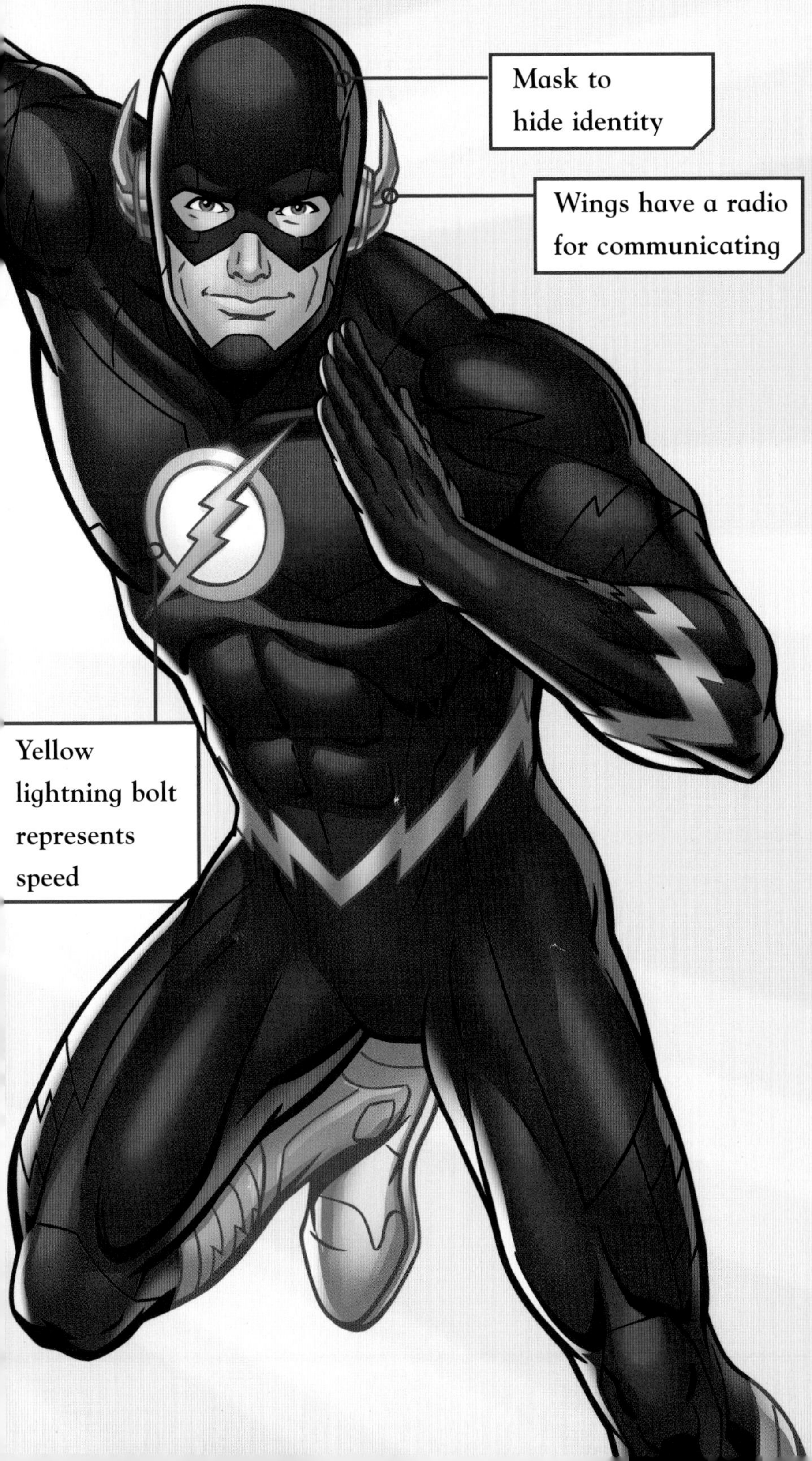
Mask to hide identity
Wings have a radio for communicating
Yellow lightning bolt represents speed

The Flash Ring

The Flash has a special ring.
It stores his costume when
he is not wearing it. Barry presses
a small button on the ring, and
his suit shoots out. He can change
into it at super-speed. The ring
also has a lightning bolt on it,
just like his costume.

The Flash Ring

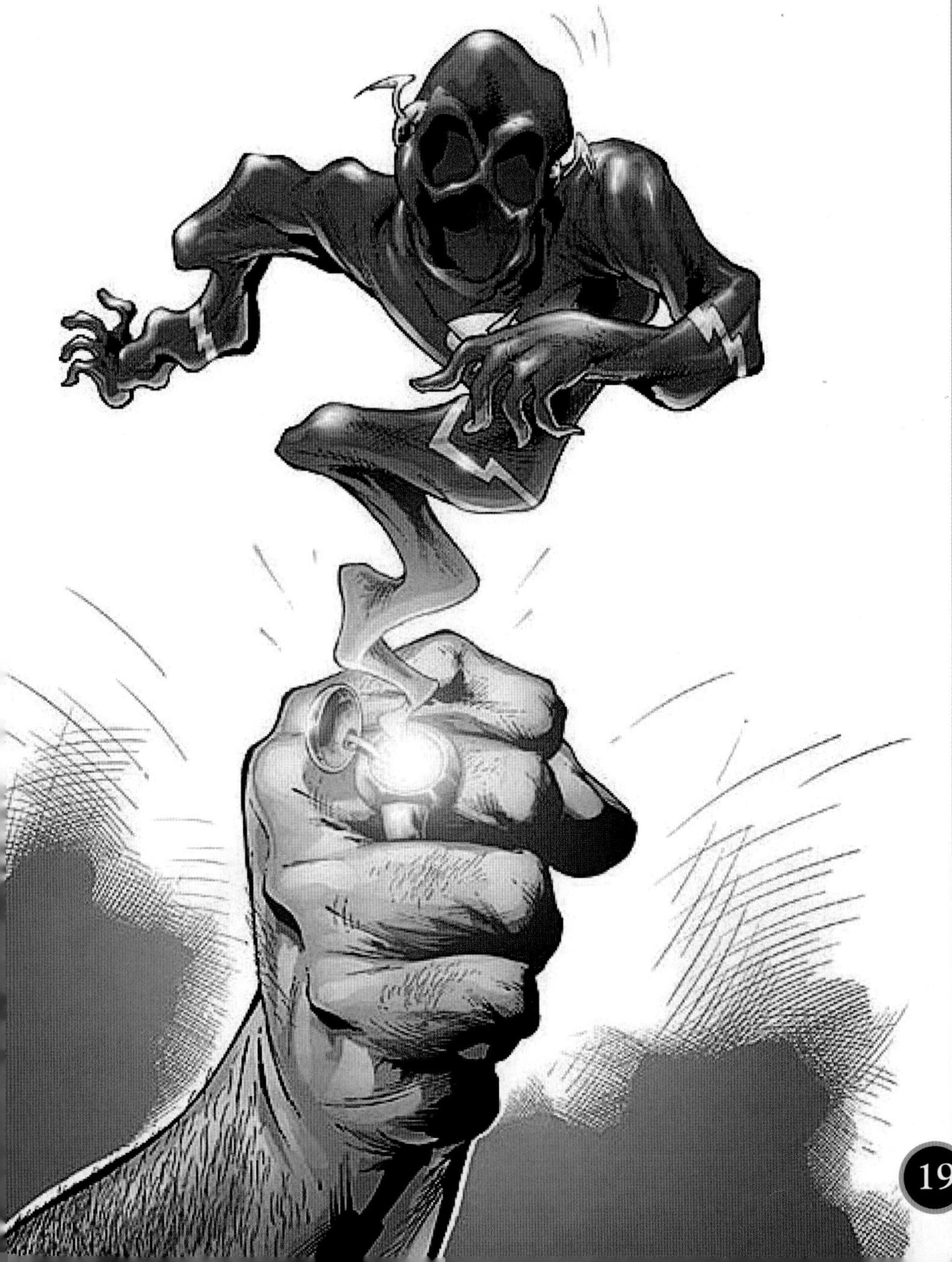

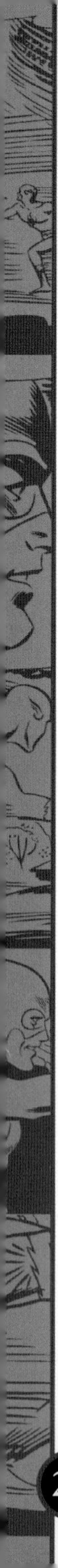

Not the first Flash

Barry Allen is not the first Super Hero to call himself The Flash. The first was a man named Jay Garrick. He also has super-speed powers. He lives in Keystone City.

Barry and Jay have teamed up many times to fight crime in Central City and Keystone City.

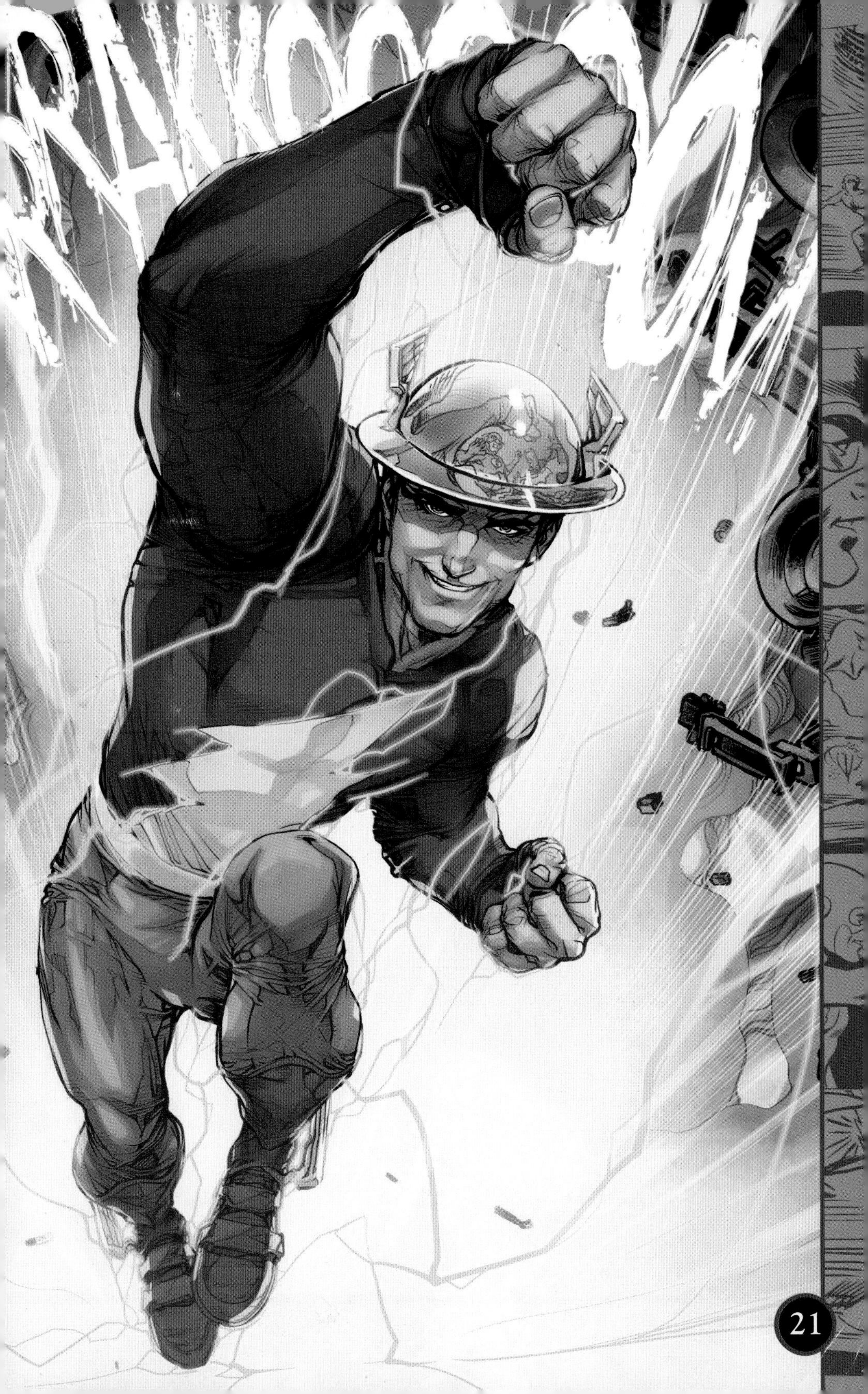

Iris West

Iris West is Barry's girlfriend. She is a reporter for Picture News in Central City.

Barry keeps his Super Hero identity a secret from Iris at first. She learns Barry is The Flash when she hears him talking in his sleep.

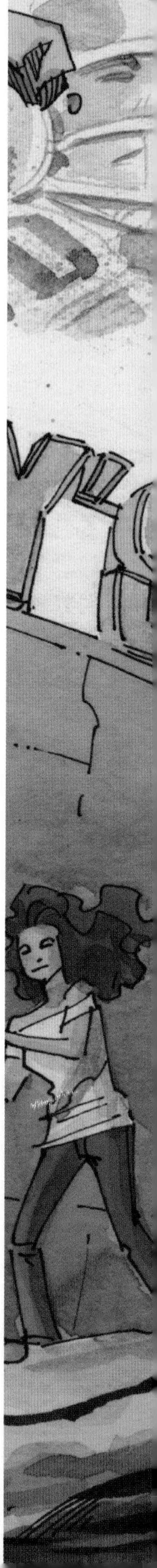

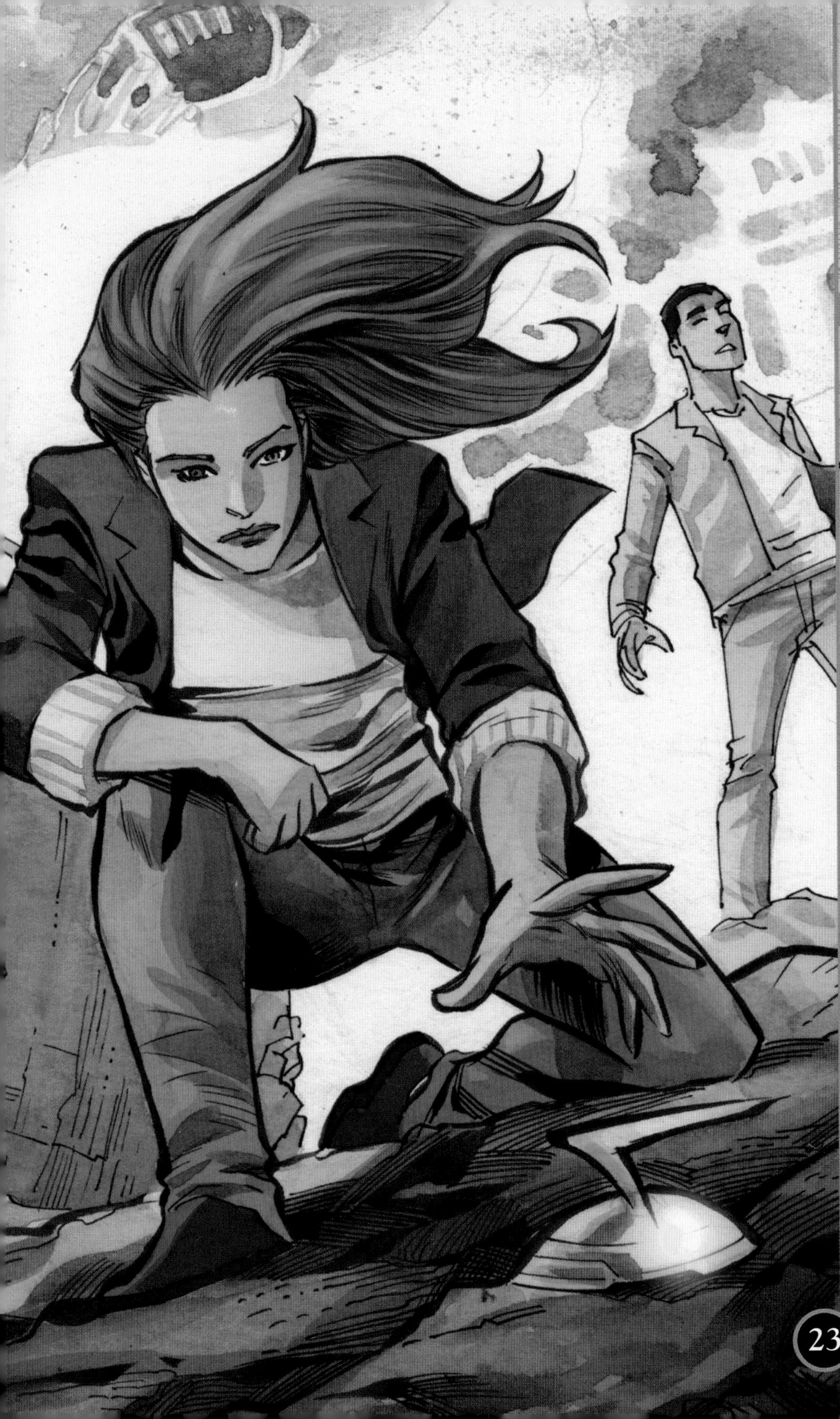

Kid Flash

Wally West is Iris's nephew. His hero is The Flash. Barry explains to Wally how The Flash got his superpowers. Wally wishes he could have superpowers.

During a storm, Wally is covered in the same chemicals that gave The Flash his powers. Now Wally has speed powers, too. He calls himself Kid Flash.

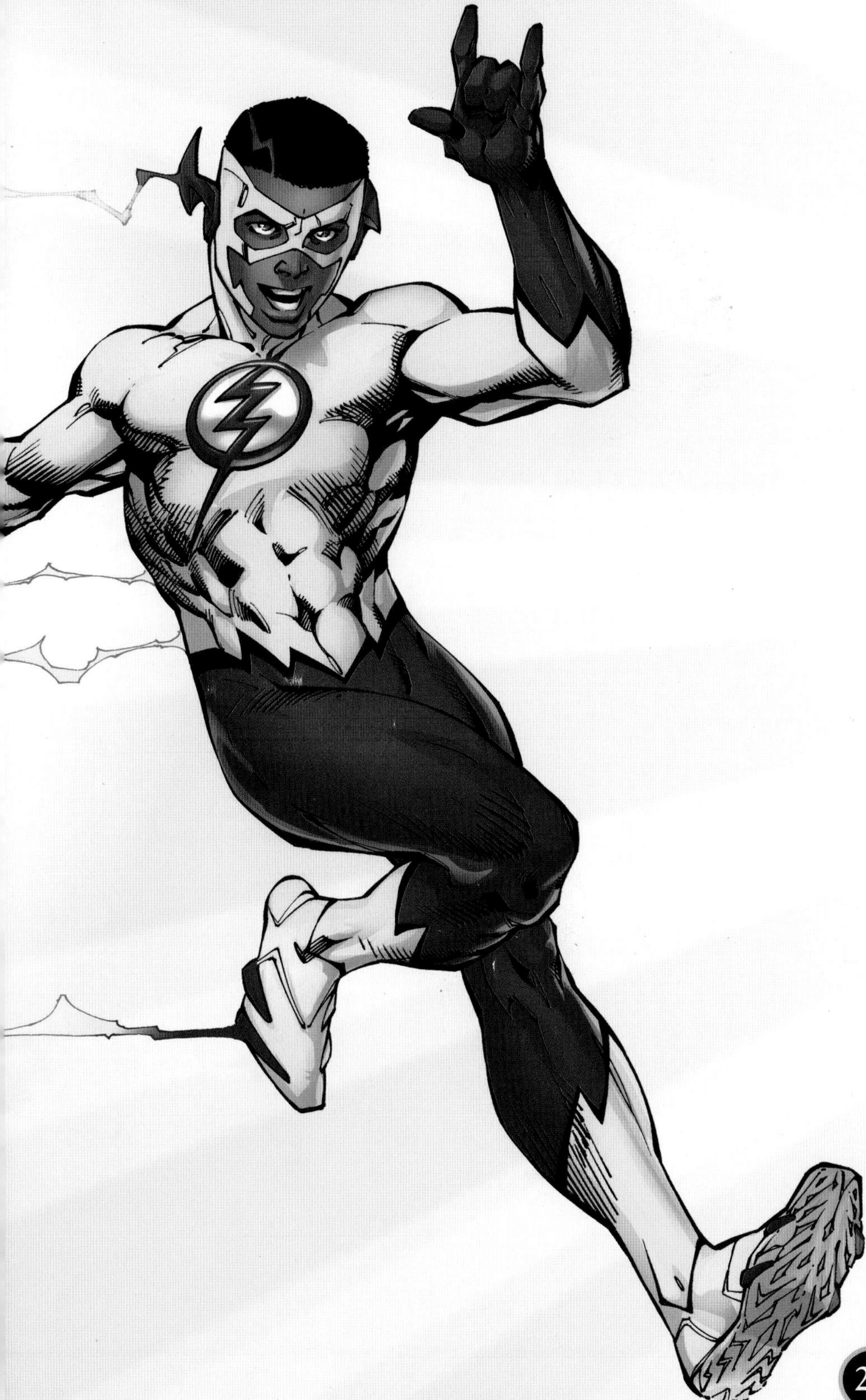

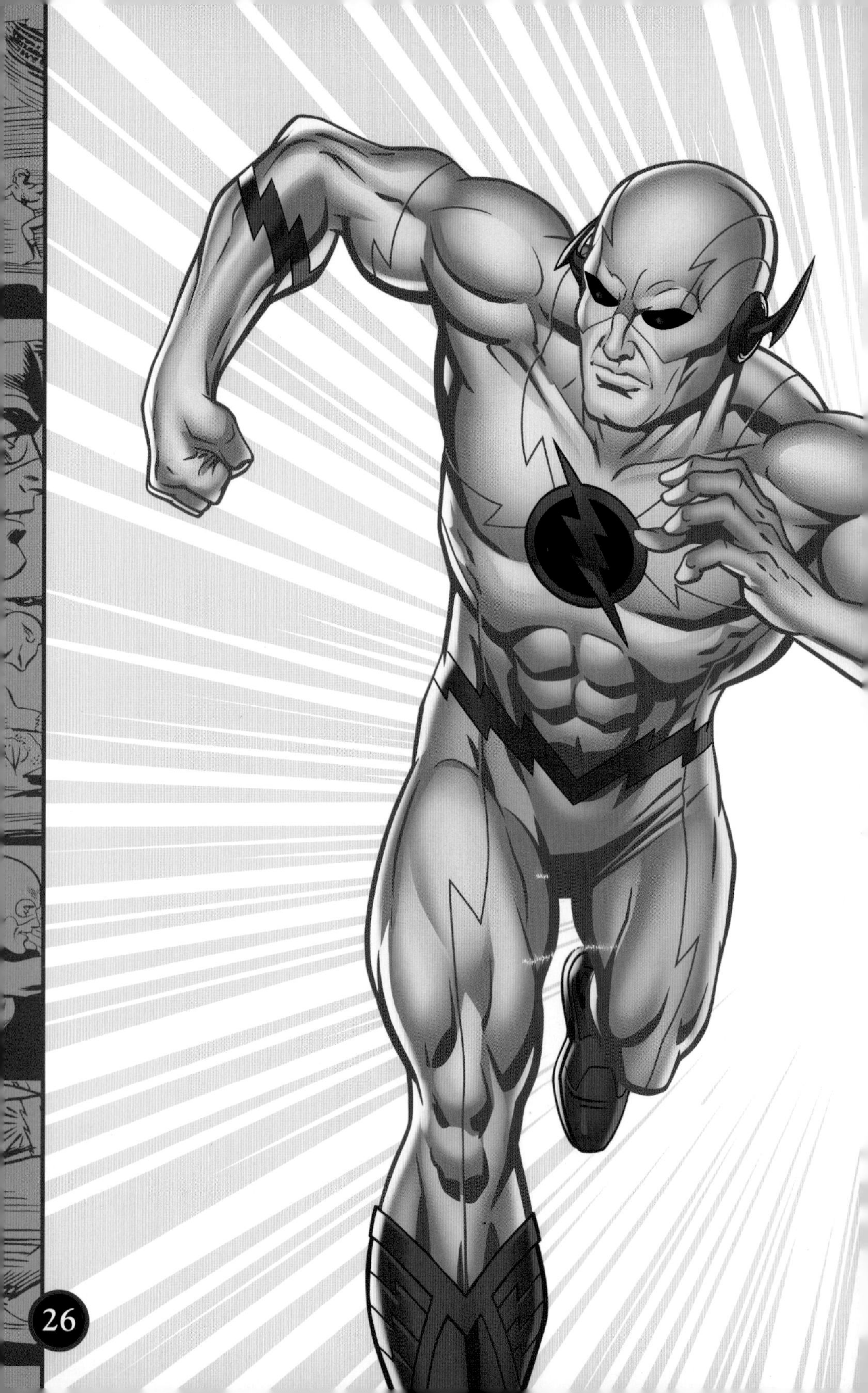

Reverse-Flash

Eobard Thawne is a time-traveler from the 25th century. He knows a lot about the Speed Force. He calls himself the Reverse-Flash.

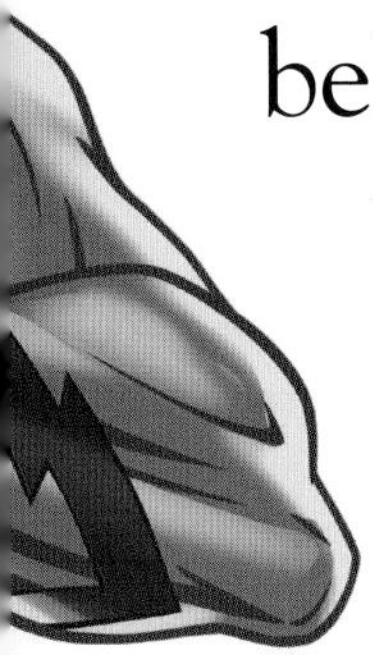

He wears a costume that once belonged to The Flash, but he has changed the color of it to yellow. The costume gives him super-speed.

Reverse-Flash hates Barry Allen and travels through time to battle him again and again.

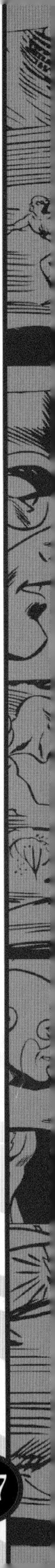

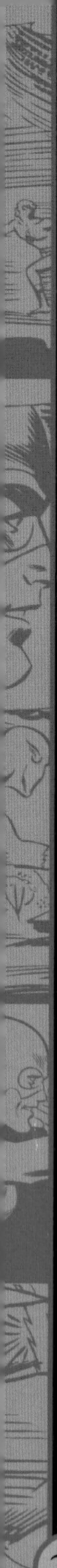

Captain Cold and The Rogues

Captain Cold is one of The Flash's worst enemies. He can fire blasts of ice that stop people in their tracks.

Captain Cold is the leader of the Rogues. The Rogues are a team of super-villains. They can't often defeat The Flash alone, but together they are much more powerful.

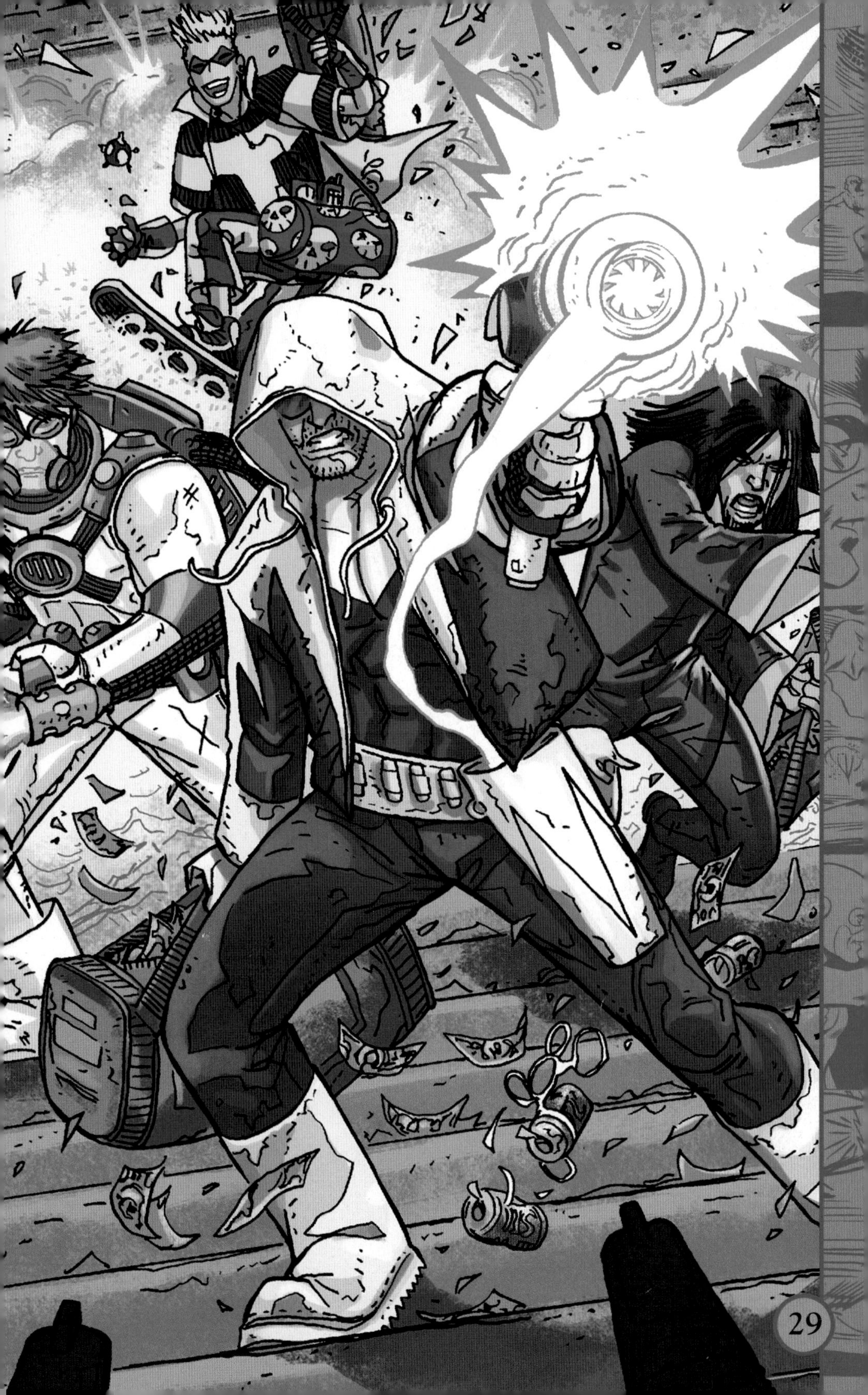

Heat Wave and Weather Wizard

The super-villain Heat Wave uses a flamethrower that can melt The Flash's boots. He wears a special suit that protects him from fire.

Weather Wizard stole a wand from his brother. The wand allowed him to control the weather. Now, he is so powerful that he can control the weather even without his wand. This makes him very difficult for The Flash to defeat.

Weather Wizard

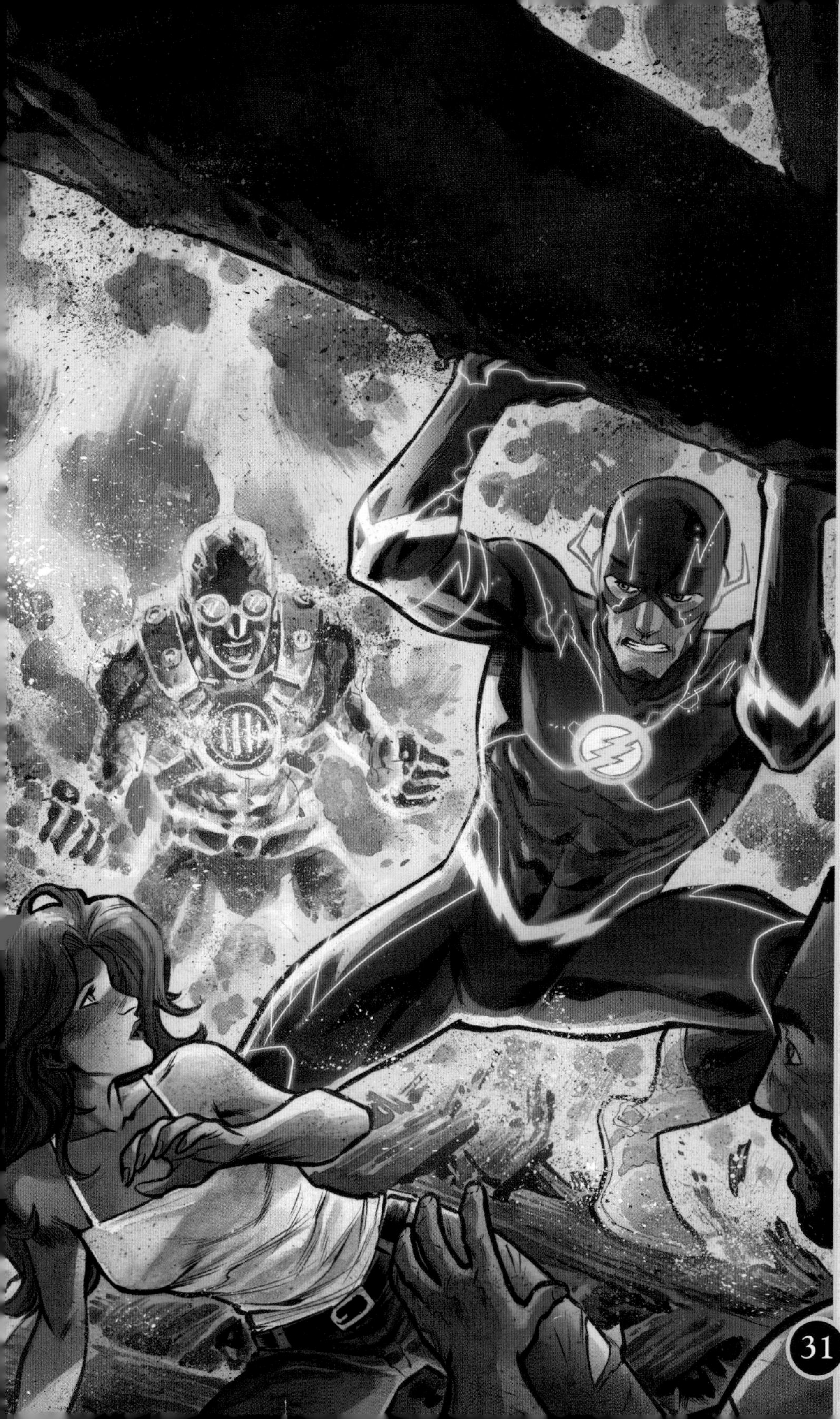

Golden Glider and Mirror Master

Golden Glider is Captain Cold's sister. She used to be a figure skater. Now she uses her ice skates as a weapon. They create their own ice, so she can skate wherever she likes.

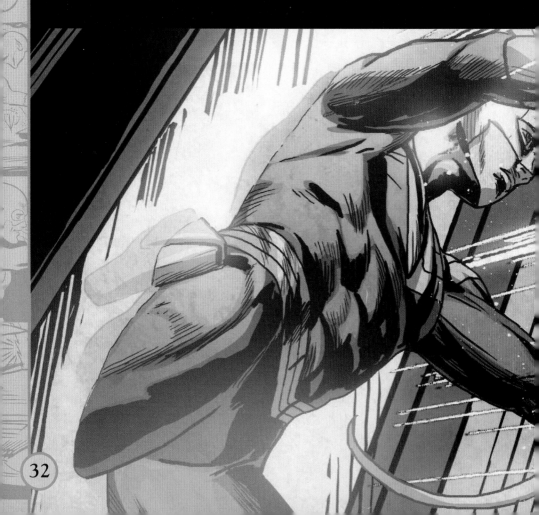

Mirror Master uses his Mirror Gun to turn things into glass. He can also use it to create lifelike illusions of huge bugs, terrifying creatures—and even himself!

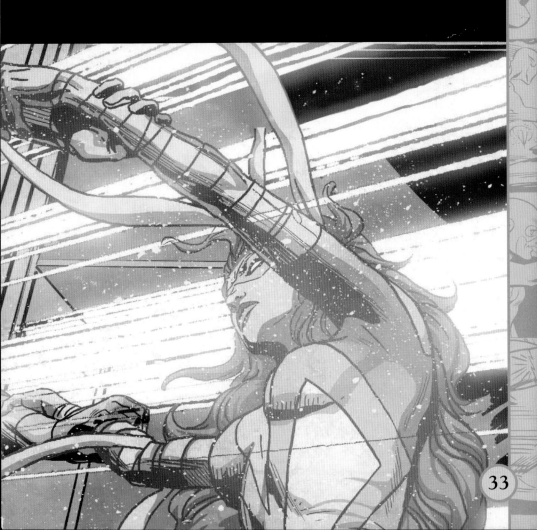

Founding the Justice League

Sometimes Super Heroes work together to fight crime and keep the world safe. The Justice League is one of the most famous Super Hero teams.

The Justice League members are all very strong and can fight their enemies alone. They are even more powerful when they work together.

The Flash is an important member of the Justice League.

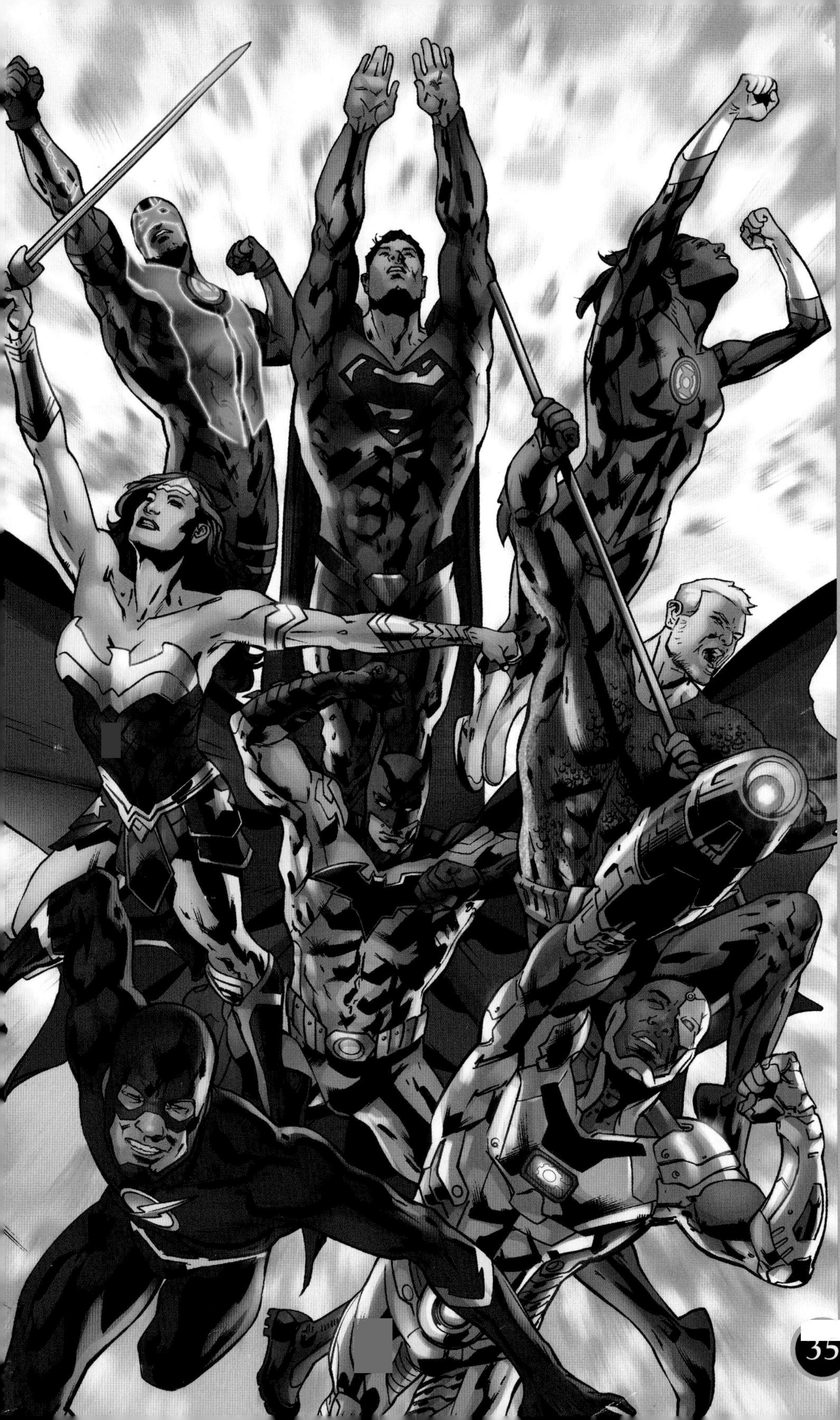

Hal Jordan

Hal Jordan is the Green
Lantern. He works for an
intergalactic police force.
Green Lantern wears a ring
that gives him his special
powers. He can travel
underwater and through
space. He can also fly.

   Green Lantern fights
alongside The Flash and
other heroes as a member
of the Justice League.

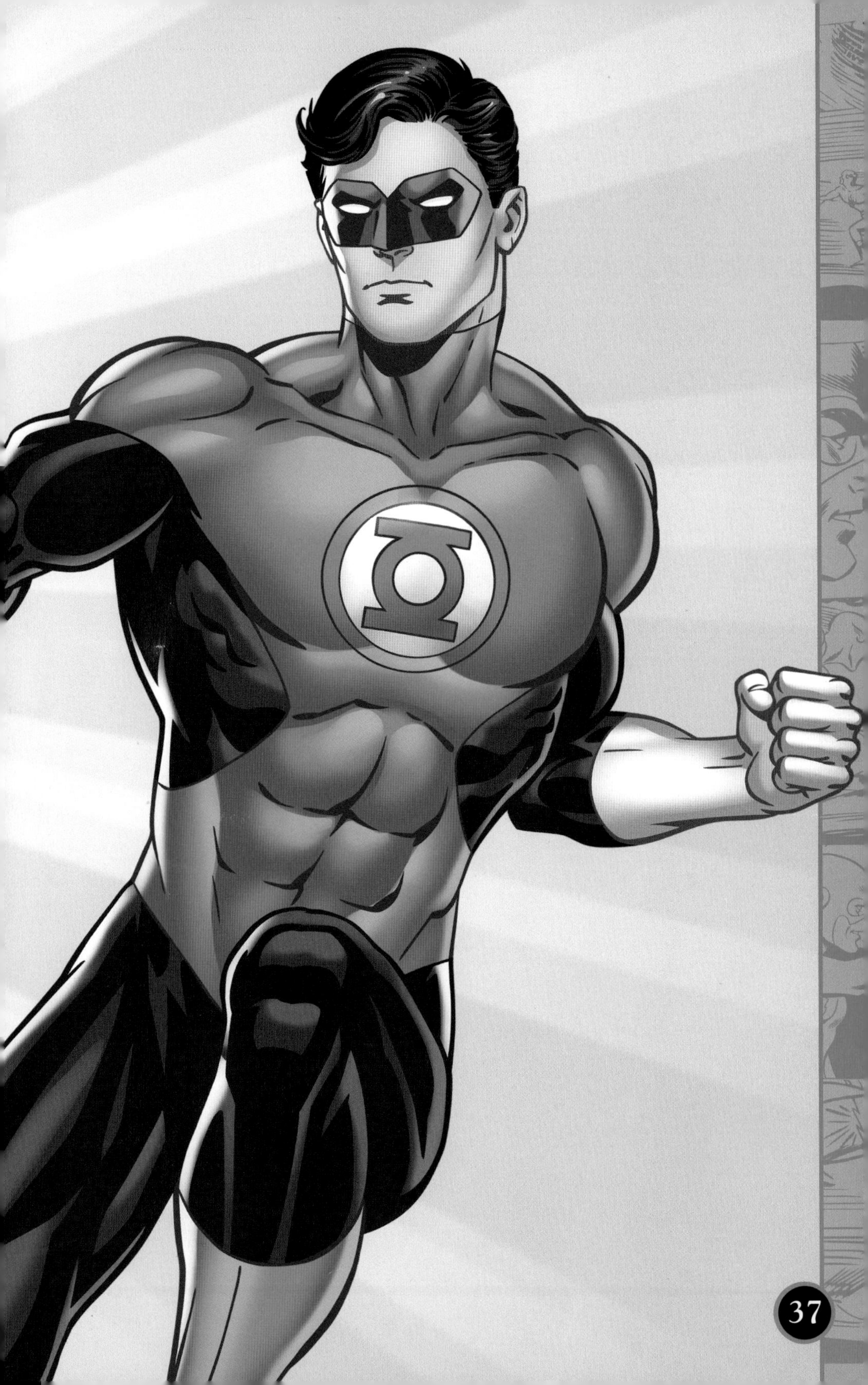

Batman

Bruce Wayne is the Super
Hero Batman. He fights
crime in Gotham City.
He does not have any
superpowers, but he uses
a lot of technology.

Batman is a founding
member of the Justice League.

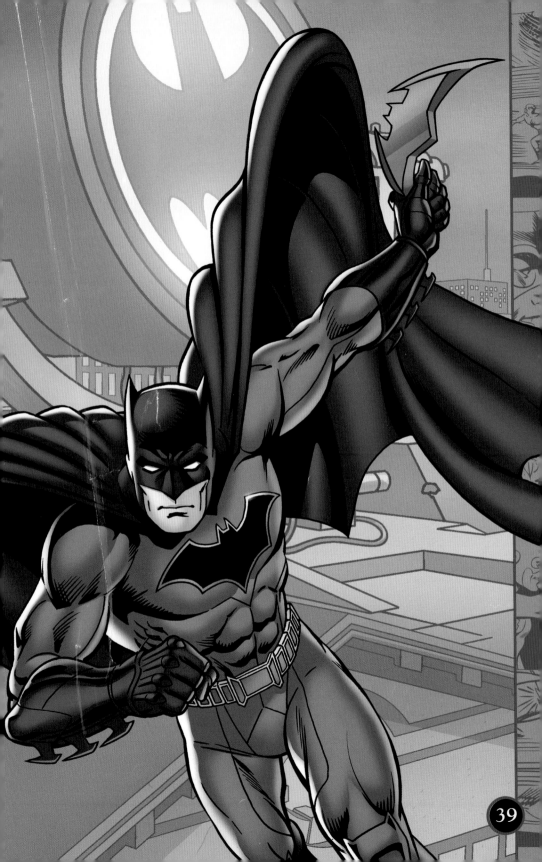

The Justice League

What's better than one Super Hero? A team of Super Heroes! Meet the other members of the Justice League.

Batman does not have superpowers, but he is a martial arts expert.

Green Lantern uses his ring to bring things in his imagination to life.

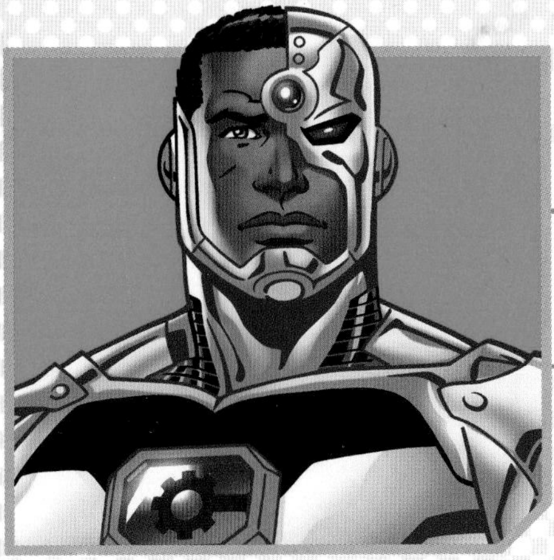

Cyborg is a genius with a very high IQ.

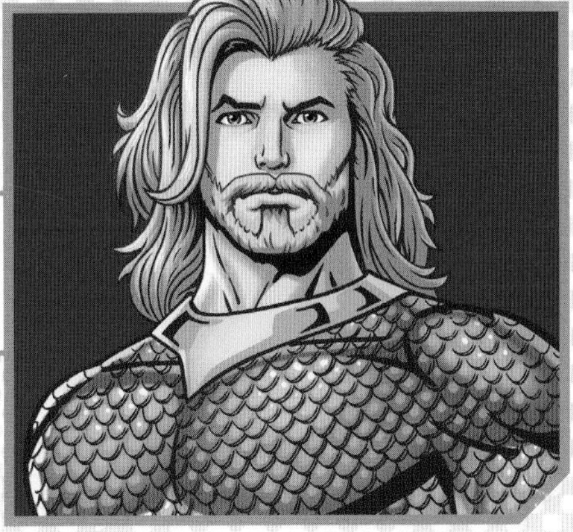

Aquaman is the King of the Seven Seas.

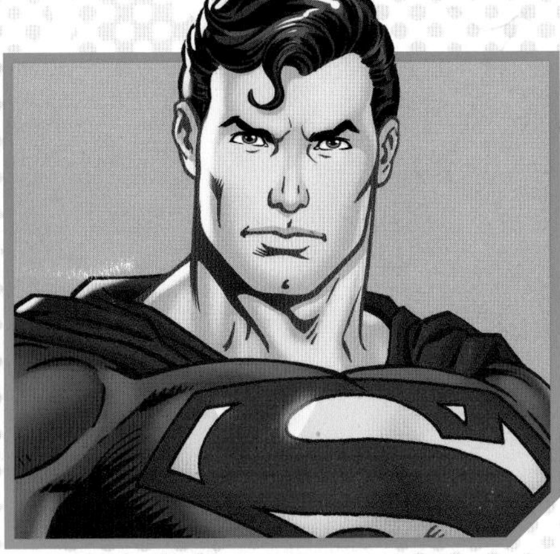

Superman is from the planet Krypton. He has super-strength and speed.

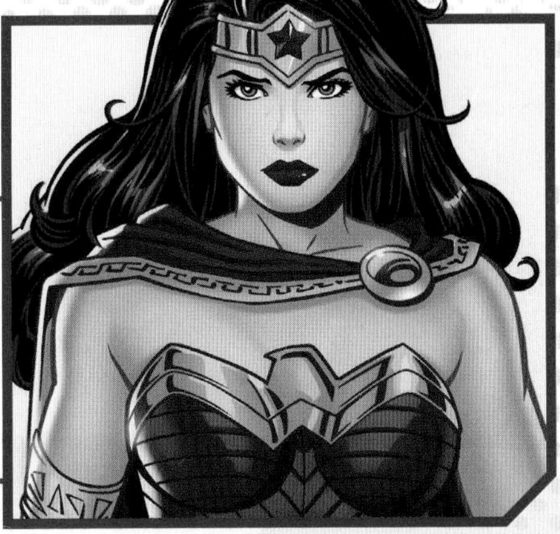

Wonder Woman has superpowers and is from the island of Themyscira.

Speedster protection

Jay Garrick, Barry Allen, and Wally West all face many challenges as The Flash.

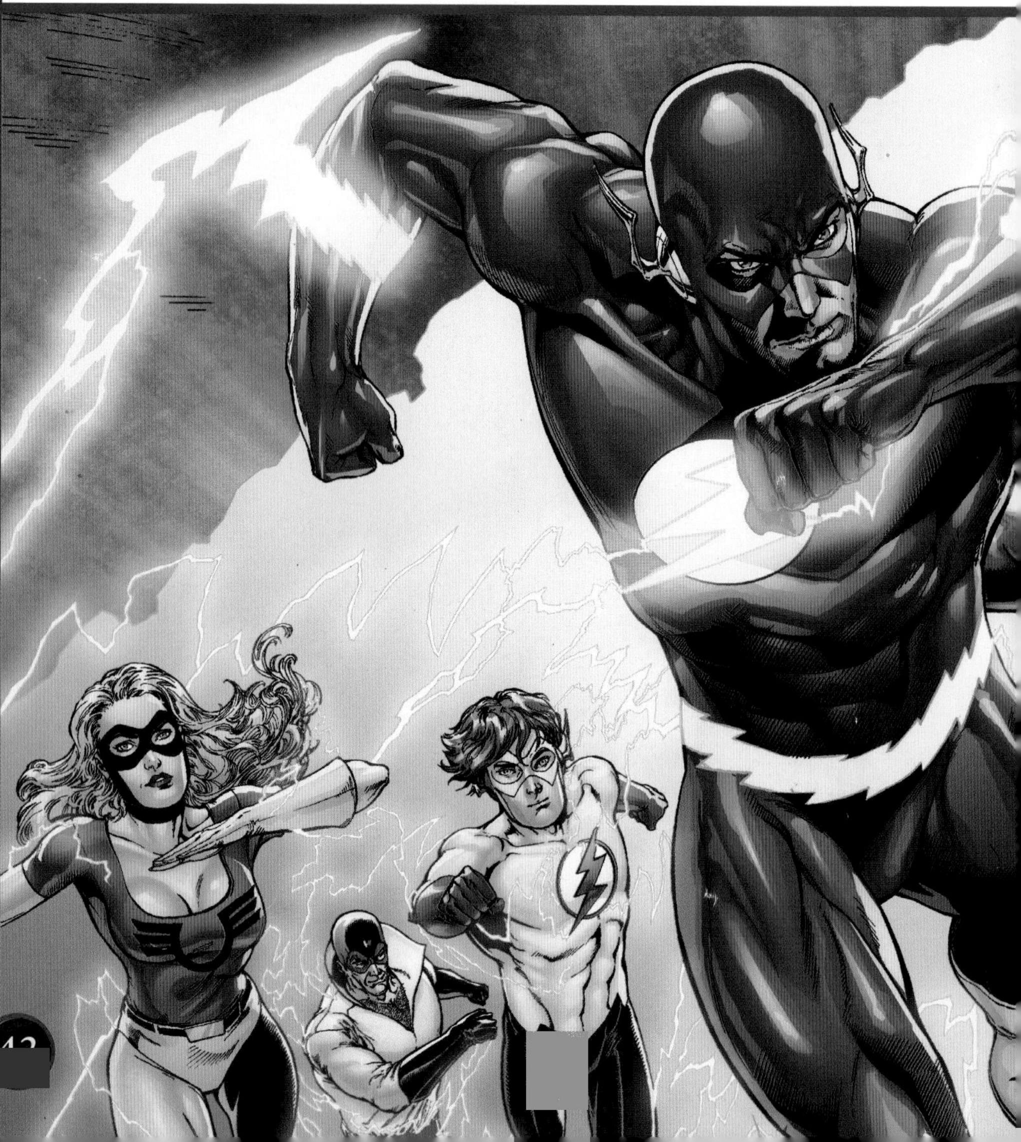

No matter who holds the title, the citizens of Earth can be sure that the Fastest Man Alive will protect them.

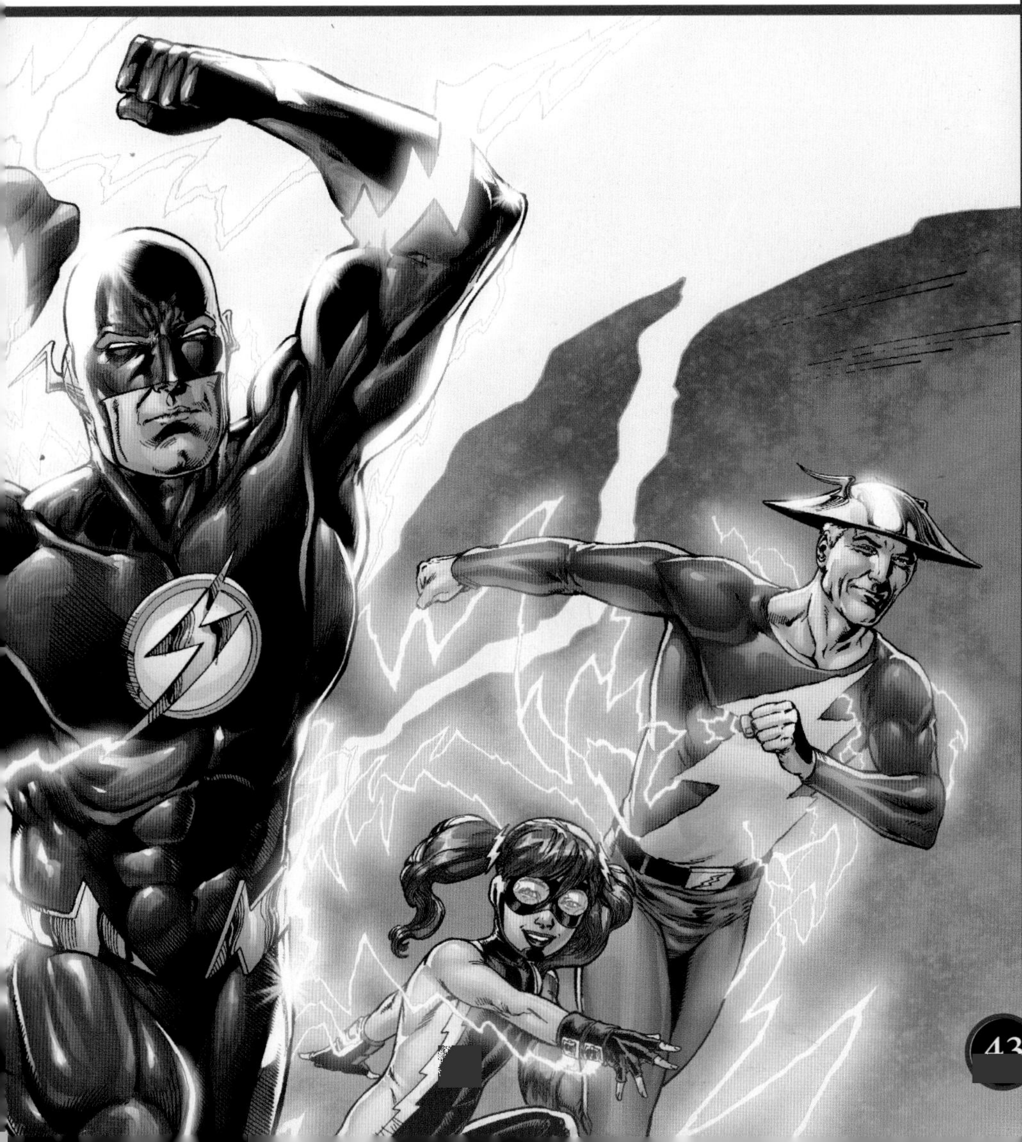

Quiz

1. What is the name of Barry Allen's girlfriend?

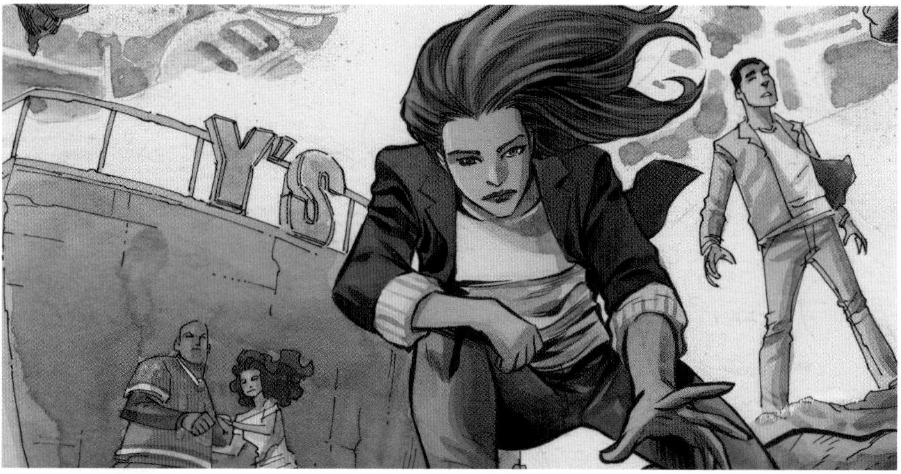
Y'S

2. Who is the leader of The Rogues?

3. True or false: Barry Allen is the only Flash.

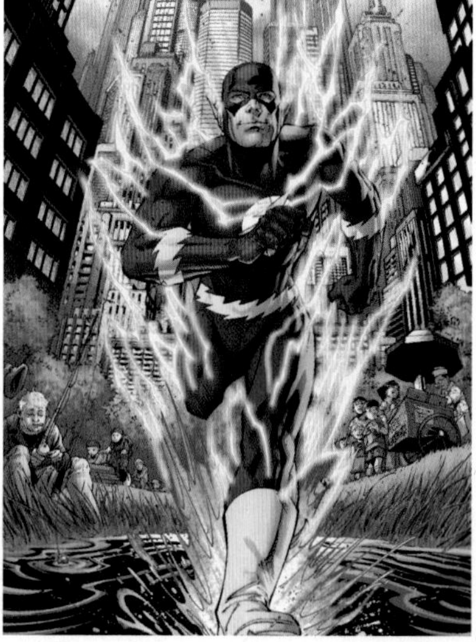

4. Where does Barry Allen live?

5. Which of The Flash's clothing items can Heat Wave melt?

6. Which member of the Justice League is the King of the Seven Seas?

7. Does Batman have any superpowers?

8. Two members of the Justice League wear a ring. One of them is The Flash. Who is the other?

9. What color is the Reverse-Flash's costume?

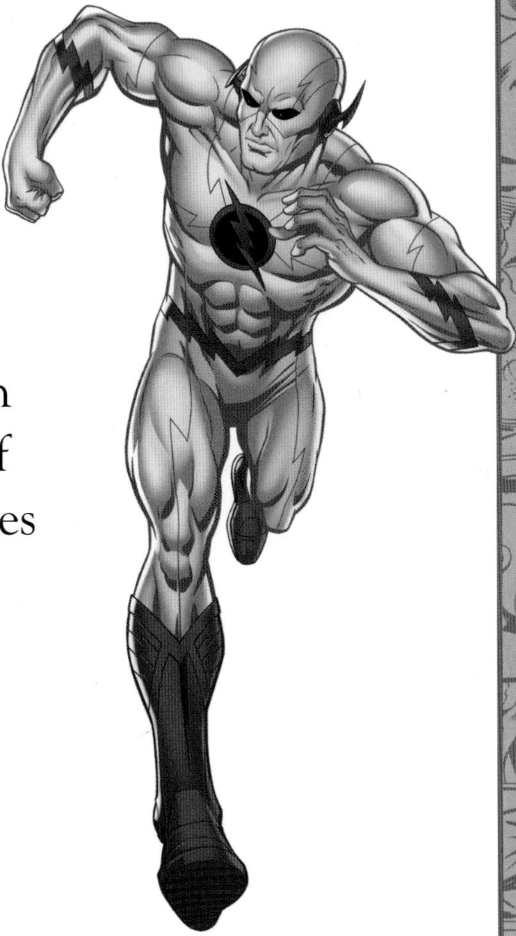

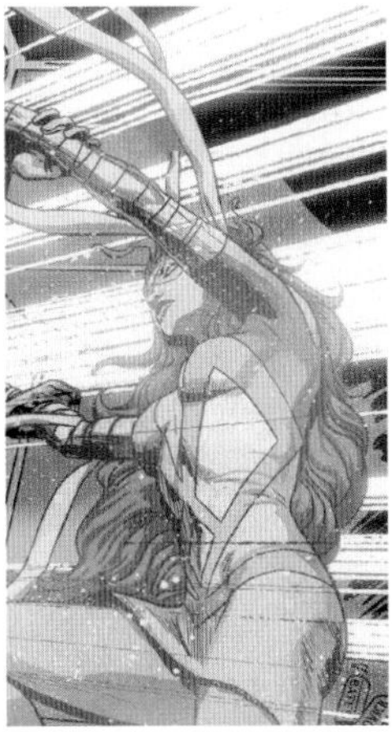

10. Which member of The Rogues used to be a figure skater?

Answers on page 47

Glossary

agility
the ability to move and think quickly and easily.

citizens
people who live in a place and call it home.

crime
an action that is against the law.

fateful
a day or event that has a big effect on the future.

flamethrower
a weapon that shoots out fire.

forensic scientist
someone who collects evidence from a crime scene and looks at it very closely to try to find clues.

founding member
someone who starts an organization or team.

illusion
something that you can see that is not real.

intergalactic
involving lots of different galaxies.

Index

Answers to the quiz on pages 44 and 45:
1. Iris West 2. Captain Cold 3. False—Jay Garrick was the first Super Hero who called himself The Flash. 4. Central City 5. His shoes 6. Aquaman 7. No 8. Green Lantern 9. Yellow 10. Golden Glider

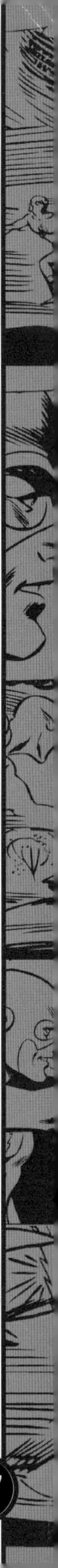

A LEVEL FOR EVERY READER

This book is a part of an exciting four-level reading series to support children in developing the habit of reading widely for both pleasure and information. Each book is designed to develop a child's reading skills, fluency, grammar awareness, and comprehension in order to build confidence and enjoyment when reading.

Ready for a Level 2 (Beginning to Read) book
A child should:
- be able to recognize a bank of common words quickly and be able to blend sounds together to make some words.
- be familiar with using beginner letter sounds and context clues to figure out unfamiliar words.
- sometimes correct his/her reading if it doesn't look right or make sense.
- be aware of the need for a slight pause at commas and a longer one at periods.

A valuable and shared reading experience
For many children, reading requires much effort, but adult participation can make reading both fun and easier. Here are a few tips on how to use this book with a young reader:

Check out the contents together:
- read about the book on the back cover and talk about the contents page to help heighten interest and expectation.
- discuss new or difficult words.
- chat about labels, annotations, and pictures.

Support the reader:
- give the book to the young reader to turn the pages.
- where necessary, encourage longer words to be broken into syllables, sound out each one, and then flow the syllables together; ask him/her to reread the sentence to check the meaning.
- encourage the reader to vary her/his voice as she/he reads; demonstrate how to do this if helpful.

Talk at the end of each book, or after every few pages:
- ask questions about the text and the meaning of the words used—this helps develop comprehension skills.
- read the quiz at the end of the book and encourage the reader to answer the questions, if necessary, by turning back to the relevant pages to find the answers.

Series consultant Dr. Linda Gambrell, Distinguished Professor of Education at Clemson University, has served as President of the National Reading Conference, the College Reading Association, and the International Reading Association.

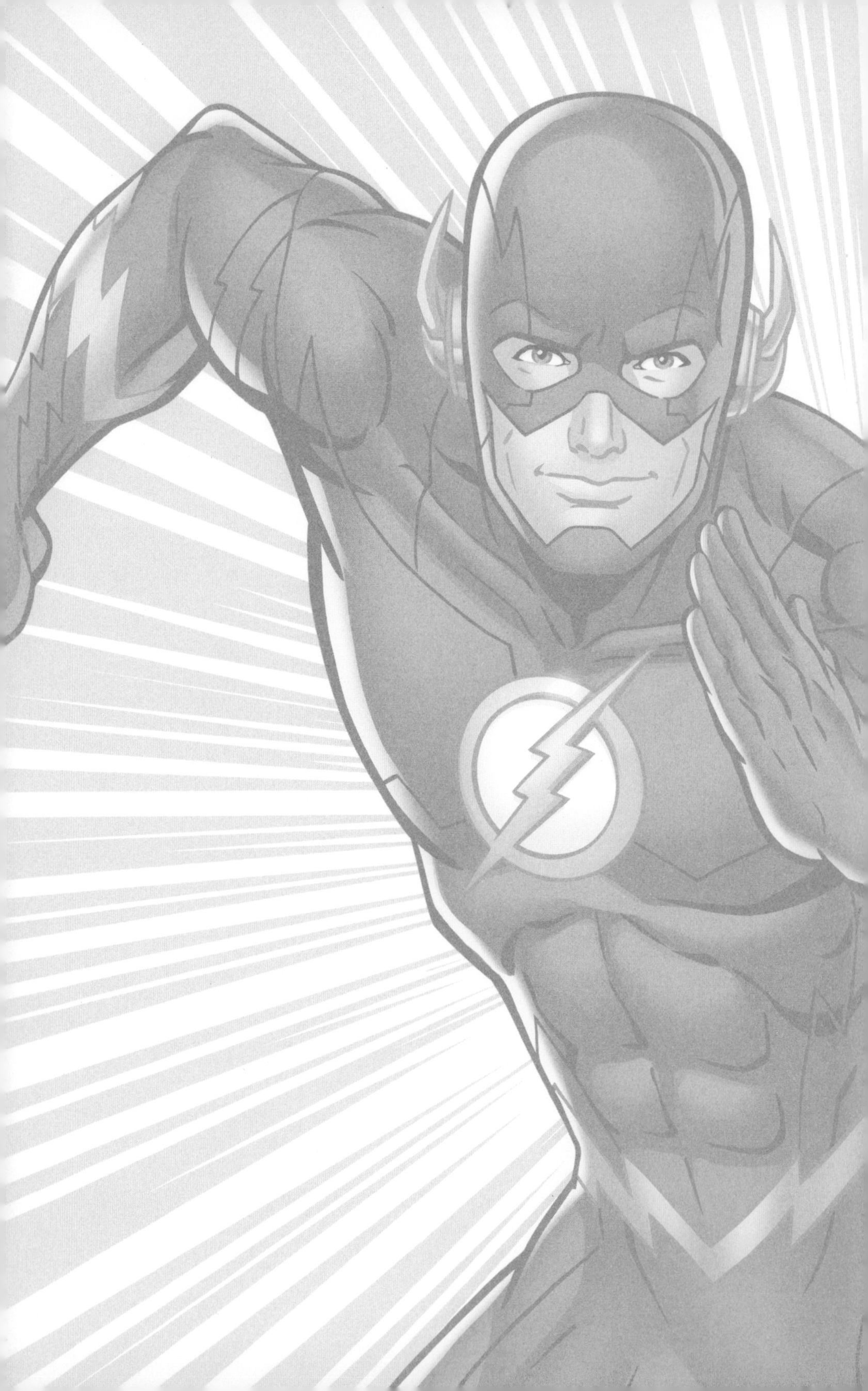